Mule
School

For Ben and Tom, with love
J.R.

To Shane
L.C.

First published in Great Britain in 2007 by
Gullane Children's Books
an imprint of Pinwheel Limited

Winchester House, 259-269 Old Marylebone Road, London NW1 5XJ

10 9 8 7 6 5 4 3 2 1

Text © Julia Rawlinson 2007 • Illustrations © Lynne Chapman 2007

The right of Julia Rawlinson and Lynne Chapman to be identified as the author and illustrator of this
work has been asserted by them in accordance with the Copyright, Designs and Patents Act, 1988.
A CIP record for this title is available from the British Library.

ISBN-13: 978-1-86233-645-2 • ISBN-10: 1-86233-645-8

Printed and bound in China

Mule
School

Julia Rawlinson

Lynne Chapman

GULLANE
CHILDREN'S BOOKS

Stomper did not like **Mule School**. He liked the other mules. He liked lunchtime and playtime. But he did not like *Stubbornness Practice*.

Every day his timetable was the same:

9 o'clock: **Stubbornness**
11 o'clock: **Kicking**
12 o'clock: **Lunch**
1 o'clock: **Stubbornness**
3 o'clock: **Kicking**
4 o'clock: **Home**

Day after day the mules recited

"Won't, won't, won't," and "Shan't, shan't, shan't."

They **SHOOK** their heads and **STAMPED** their feet.

But one day Stomper put his hoof in the air. "What if we *want* to do as we're told?" he asked nervously.

"You are a mule. Refuse!" cried Mrs Kick.

"But what if it seems like a good idea?" mumbled Stomper. **"Nobody else's idea is good,"** she snapped, and sent him to stand in the corner.

Stomper's first **stubbornness test** was to guard a pile of apples. He stood mumbling "*No, no, no,*" under his breath, but before long a scruffy pig snuffled up.

"My piglets are hungry. Could you spare some apples?" she asked. "Of course," nodded Stomper. "Help yourself."

The pig waddled happily off with
the apples, but then Stomper gulped.
He had forgotten to be stubborn.

"Fool of a mule," cried Mrs Kick.
"You must never, ever
give in to a pig."

Stomper's next task
was to block a path.

Soon a family of goats needed to
get past. Stomper stood aside and
waved them by politely . . .

But then the school's meanest mules, Biff and Bash, jumped out and laughed. *"We are mules, we like to* **kick.** *Weakness makes us* **sick, sick, sick!"** they chanted as they circled him.

"We're going to tell on you. You were meant to stop the goats, not let them through."

"They're right," thought Stomper sadly. "I am a useless mule."

"Stamper, why am I so weak?"
asked Stomper in the playground.
"You're not weak. You've got a good kick,"
said Stamper. "Come and play bash ball."

He walloped the ball over the
straw store and Stomper galloped after it,
forgetting all his stubbornness troubles as he
raced across the yard. They bashed and butted,
kicked and crashed until it was time for class.

That afternoon there was a field trip to practise kicking in the valley, but Stomper was sent out apple-picking to replace the apples he had lost.

He wandered up the valley side, following a butterfly, and was listening to the mules chanting below when he heard another sound.

The dam up the valley had...

BUR

ST!

And a great river was roaring down. His friends were going to be . . .

swept away!

"MOVE!"

cried Stomper, as loudly
as he could, but the mules
didn't hear him.

"Leaf or branch
or rock or stick,
whatever it is
we'll give it a . . .

kick!"

they chanted,
far below.

"RUN!"

thundered Stomper, waving
his hooves wildly, but
the mules were not looking.

"Nose to the ground
and tail to the sky,
let those thundering
mule hooves . . .

fly!"

they cried as they
kick-kick-kicked.

Then, at last, Mrs Kick saw the water
swooshing towards her. She faced up the valley,
dug in her hooves, bared her teeth and cried,

**"We are mules and we won't budge,
even for an . . .**

ENORMOUS FLOOD!"

The other mules took
up the cry. Their eyes
were wide, their ears were
back, but their trembling
hooves were planted
firmly in the mud.

Suddenly another sound rose above the rushing water.

CRASH!

CRASH!

CRASH!

The mules screwed their
eyes tight shut and covered
their heads with their
hooves, but then . . .

"IT'S STOMPER!"

cried Stamper with a mighty neigh of delight. Stomper's head was down, his heels were flying and he was **kick-kick-kicking** with all his might.

CR

CRASH

CRA

CRASH!

He kicked at rocks, he kicked at
sticks, he kicked at broken branches.
Wood and rock tumbled down the
valley side with a rumbling roar,
making a new dam that whooshed
the water safely away.

Stomper trotted down the hill and stood, casually
nibbling flowers. Slowly the other mules sidled up.
"We were wrong," they muttered, "we were foolish mules."

Stomper shook his head.
"No," he said, "you stood your
ground. You did what a mule should
do. It's just lucky that not all mules
are exactly the same as you."

Mrs Kick looked thoughtful as
she led them back to school.

Next day at Mule School the timetable read:

9 o'clock: **Stubbornness or Pottery**

11 o'clock: **Kicking or Flower Arranging**

12 o'clock: **Lunch**

1 o'clock: **Stubbornness or Hoof Printing**

3 o'clock: **Kicking or Musical Mules**

4 o'clock: **Home**

And at 11 o'clock, while Stomper
happily kicked his way through class . . .

...Biff and Bash were down
in the meadow, merrily
arranging daisies.